MIKE'S HOUSE

MIKE'S HOUSE

BY JULIA L. SAUER

ILLUSTRATED BY DON FREEMAN

THE VIKING PRESS
New York

PIC BK 1. LIBRARIES—FICTION

LITHOGRAPHED IN THE UNITED STATES OF AMERICA BY AFFILIATED LITHOGRAPHERS

To

Eunice Gates Mullan,

so loved,

so wise in opening doors

to little girls and boys

ROBERT was four years old. For a whole year, ever since he was three, he had gone to the Picture Book Hour at the public library every Tuesday morning.

When Robert reached the library, with its big front doors and hall of shining marble, the first thing he did was to say "good morning" to Mr. Noble. Mr. Noble was always smiling, and he always stood behind a little desk just inside the door. And Mr. Noble always shook his head and said the same thing.

"My, my! Tough boys and girls, these pre-schoolers! It's never too cold or too hot or too snowy or too rainy for *them* to come to the library."

Robert always smiled back proudly, and he strutted
just a little because Mr. Noble made him feel grown up.

Robert liked the Picture Book Hour; he liked Phyllis and Norman and Jackie and Carl and all the other girls and boys who came every Tuesday; and he liked Mrs. Mullan, who showed them the pictures in the books and told them the stories. She had such a pleasant voice. There were little laughs just around the corners in it. But best of all Robert liked what came *after* the stories.

Then he might choose a book to take home and keep for a whole week.

Robert always wanted the same book. That book was *Mike Mulligan and His Steam Shovel*. The steam shovel's name was Mary Anne, and Robert thought that was very funny. Of all the books in Mrs. Mullan's room Robert liked *Mike Mulligan* best, and he wanted *Mike Mulligan* on *every* Tuesday.

Mother would say patiently, "But, Robert, you know *Mike Mulligan* by heart now."

Mrs. Mullan would say patiently, "It would be nice to let Carl or Harold take *Mike* this week, Robert."

If Robert felt good and pleasant he would take another book just to please them. But if he felt cross and a little bad inside he would stick out his lip and stalk off, leaving Mother to follow with some other book.

Robert was quite sure that Mike was his best friend. And because he loved Mike so very much Robert thought that the whole library had been built as a house for Mike. He always called the library "Mike's house." He never said, "I'm going to the library." He always said, "I'm going to Mike's house."

One Tuesday when Robert woke up it was blowing
and blustering outside. The windows rattled and the
trees tossed their branches.

"It's a real blizzard, Robert. Don't you think we
had better stay home today?" Mother asked.

Robert shook his head. "Oh *no*," he said. "You remember, Mother, Mr. Noble at Mike's house says preschool boys and girls are *tough*. I can't stay home because it's a blizzard."

Mother laughed and said, "If you're that tough I guess I'll have to be tough too. I'll hurry with my work so we'll be on time."

But even though Mother hurried they were a little late. At the corner nearest to Mike's house Mother stopped the car and let Robert get out.

"You run down to Mike's house and go straight in, Robert. You mustn't be late. I'll pick you up as usual after Picture Book Hour."

15

Just as Mother drove off a big wind came whistling up behind Robert. It shoved him around; it snatched off his red cap and went whistling down the street, tossing the red cap in the air and catching it when it came down.

Robert ran after it. A whole block down the street
he ran. The wind had dropped his cap, and he could
see it lying on the sidewalk. But just as he stooped to
pick it up the wind gave another shrill whistle and
sent it spinning away from him down the sidewalk
like a bright red top.

Robert had to stand still and laugh. He was still
laughing, "Ho! ho! ho!" all by himself, when a big boy
came up to him with the runaway cap in his hand.

"This yours, kid?" he asked.

"Yes," Robert said, "it got away from me."

"So I see," said the big boy, and he jammed the cap down hard over Robert's ears.

"Hang on to it," he said, and hardly waited for Robert to thank him.

And then Robert looked around. There was a candy
store and a paint store and a store with horses' harness
in the window. But there was no Mike's house any-
where in sight! Robert looked up the street; he looked
down the street; he looked across the street. *He didn't
know where he was.* He turned round and round and
round. Then he stood perfectly still and thought hard.

What was it that Mother had told him to do if he was lost? Of course! He was to look for a policeman! So Robert looked up the street and down the street. But before he saw a policeman he heard a big cheerful voice booming out, "Wait for me, young fellow! Wait for me, young fellow!"

The big voice came closer and closer. Robert saw a shiny police car sliding along the curb toward him. The big voice came from the loudspeaker on top, and it was talking to *him!* He ran to the curb when the car stopped and a big policeman got out.

"How'd you know I wanted you?" Robert asked the
policeman.

"Oh, I watched you blow down the street," the big officer said, "and then I saw you turn round and round like a pinwheel, and I said to myself, 'Business for you, Jensen! Get going!' Now tell me, sonny, what's your name?"

"Robert Austin."

"Robert Austin," the officer repeated. He wrote it down in a little book.

"And I suppose they call you Bobbie?"

"Oh no," Robert told him in a shocked voice. "I'm *Robert*."

"Good," said the officer. "Fine manly name, Robert. Know where you live?"

"One-three-four Gorsline Street," Robert said.

"Good" said the officer again, and he wrote that in his notebook. "If you know where you live you're not very *much* lost. Now tell me, Robert, where were you going?"

"To Mike's house," Robert told him promptly. "And my Mother's going too, after she parks the car."

"Mike's house," said Officer Jensen. "Hm-m-m. Happen to know this Mike's other name?"

"Oh yes," said Robert. "It's Mulligan."

"Good!" said the policeman. "Now suppose we just step into Rocco's Grill here for a minute so I can use the telephone."

He took Robert's hand, and they went into a lovely place. It looked just like a street car.

A pretty waitress with lots of yellow curls laughed when she saw the big policeman and Robert.

"Big haul, I see," she said.

The policeman and Robert laughed too.

"This is my friend Robert, Lillian," the officer said. "Hot milk for two, please, while I use the phone."

The waitress put a glass of hot milk down on the counter for Robert and a cup of coffee for the policeman.

"But he said hot milk for *two*," Robert said.

"That's just his little joke, Robert," Lillian answered. "Now drink yours quick. It'll thaw you out."

The hot milk was making him feel all comfortable inside when Officer Jensen came back from the telephone booth.

"Nobody answers at your house, Robert," he said, "so I can't take you straight home."

"I know," Robert said. "My father's at work and my mother's parking the car."

"I see," said the policeman. "We'll have to work on this Mike Mulligan clue then. Only his name's not in the phone book. Tell me, sonny, is—is Mr. Mulligan a friend of your father's?"

"Well," Robert said slowly, "Father *used* to like him, but he says he's tired of him now."

"I see," said the policeman again. "But what I mean is, he *is* a grownup, isn't he? Not just a youngster?"

"Oh yes, he's a grownup." Robert was very sure about that.

"And does he live alone?"

"No, he lives with Mary Anne," Robert told him.

"What's his house like?" the policeman wanted to know.

"It's very big," Robert explained. "You go up steps and steps and steps to the front door. And inside there are two big vases without any flowers in them. And then you go up in the elevator to the room where Mike is."

"Whew," said the policeman. He tugged at the collar of his tunic. "Come here a minute, Lillian," he called to the waitress.

"Lillian, do you know of any house like this around here?" he asked. "This Mr. Mulligan sounds like a big shot. Tell Lillian what kind of house your friend lives in, Robert."

And Robert said again, "You go up steps and steps

and steps to the front door. And inside there are two big vases without any flowers in them. And—"

"Wait a minute, Robert," Lillian interrupted. "If there aren't flowers in those vases, what *is* in them?"

"Just sand," Robert said, "so people can put their cigarettes out."

The policeman tugged at his collar again.

All at once Lillian began to laugh. "The only house around here that sounds anything like that is the public library," she said.

Robert took his last swallow of milk and put his glass down. He nodded solemnly at Lillian. "That's where Mike Mulligan lives," he said. "In the library."

The policeman gulped his whole cup of coffee down in one big swallow. Then he said to Robert, "Let me get this straight, Robert. Your friend Mike Mulligan lives in the public library?"

"Yes," Robert said. "He lives in a book in the library. Do you know where that is?"

"Well, I can find it," the policeman said with a big laugh. "And we'd better get going. This friend of yours —this Mike Mulligan—he must be a regular guy. I sure want to meet him."

"You'll love him," Robert said as he swung the policeman's big hand. "He'll be your friend too."

They went around the corner and up the block to the library. Picture Book Hour was over, and they met all the children coming out. But Robert didn't care. This was a big day—a very big day for him. And he was sure that meeting Mike Mulligan would make it a big day for Officer Jensen too.